the TREASURE of PELICAN COVE

Milly Howard

journeyforth®

Greenville, South Carolina

The Treasure of Pelican Cove

Edited by Laurie Garner
Cover and illustrations by Tom Halverson

© 1988 by BJU Press
Greenville, South Carolina 29614
JourneyForth Books is a division of BJU Press

Printed in the United States of America

ISBN 978-0-89084-464-9

35   34   33   32   31   30   29   28   27   26   25   24   23   22   21

To Jonathan, my Jimmy

Books by Milly Howard

These Are My People
Brave the Wild Trail
Captive Treasure
On Yonder Mountain
The Mystery of Pelican Cove

Crimebusters Inc.
The Case of the Dognapped Cat
The Case of the Sassy Parrot

PUBLISHER'S NOTE

A summer at grandmother's house is special for any child, and when grandmother lives on an island, it becomes a time of delight. Each summer, Jimmy and his brother and sister explore the beach and collect treasures to line the shelves in their rooms. In the process, they learn much—about the sea, about God, and about themselves—from the wisdom of both Granny and the caretaker, Hiram.

This particular summer thrusts them into an adventure that includes a kidnaped dog and a pirate's treasure, and they find themselves in the midst of problems involving suspicion and trust, greed and honor. Under the godly guidance of their grandmother, however, the children find many of their attitudes about people and events changing. And when Jimmy is faced with a final decision, he makes it with the confidence born of true character.

Contents

Chapter One

Land's End, Here We Come!

Jimmy walked with a bounce. Up and down. Up and down. At the top of each bounce, he looked around the airport. "I'll be the first to see Granny this time," he thought.

"Stop bouncing, Jimmy," Elizabeth Anne whispered. "You look like a slap-happy frog!"

"No, I don't," Jimmy said. He kept on bouncing. Mama had said to obey Elizabeth Anne on the plane. She hadn't said anything about obeying her at the airport.

"Jimmy!" Paul grabbed at Jimmy's flapping shirttail.

Jimmy dodged and quickly bounced away. Elizabeth Anne might fuss and leave it at that. Paul wouldn't. Jimmy got in one last big bounce before Paul jerked him down.

"There she is!" Jimmy yelled. "Granny! Granny! Over here!"

The other passengers grinned. They moved aside as Jimmy made a beeline for a gray-haired lady. He dragged Paul along behind him. Elizabeth Anne followed, her face pink with embarrassment.

"Jimmy!" Granny gave the freckle-faced boy a big hug. "And Paul! Careful there," she said as Paul let go of Jimmy's shirt and stumbled into her.

"Sorry, Gran," Paul said, righting himself. "Jimmy got away from me."

"I saw," Granny said. "In a hurry to get to Land's End, aren't you, Jimmy?"

"Yes'm," Jimmy said, beaming. "Is Blackie okay? Did he miss me? Did he like the bone I sent him for Christmas?"

"Blackie's just fine for a dog his age," Granny said. "And yes, I'm sure he'll remember you.

Just don't you forget that Blackie is no spring chicken."

Jimmy stopped, puzzled. "He's not a chicken at all, Granny."

"She means he's getting old," Paul said, rubbing Jimmy's hair.

Jimmy wiggled away. "I knew that."

"Here's Elizabeth Anne," Granny said. She held out both hands. "Let me look at you."

Elizabeth Anne stood still.

"My, you've become quite a lady," Granny said. Her eyes misted. "You look just like your mother did at your age."

Jimmy stared at Elizabeth Anne. He frowned. She looked just like Elizabeth Anne. He opened his mouth to say so. Paul stuck an elbow in his ribs.

"Ow!" Jimmy grunted.

"Is Hiram still at Land's End?" Paul asked.

"Still there," Granny said, "and still just as ornery as ever."

Paul grinned. Hiram was a good caretaker, but he had a mind of his own. He and Granny disagreed on just about everything except his work. His work was better than anyone else's on the island. Granny couldn't fire him if she wanted to. And she didn't want to.

"I'm glad," Jimmy said. "I like Hiram."

"So do I, son," Granny said. "Couldn't get along without him. But sometimes . . . well, some things are better left unsaid."

She took them to get their bags. Then they followed her outside. She stopped beside a faded pickup.

"Had to borrow Hiram's pickup," Granny explained. "The car's in the shop."

Granny climbed into the front seat and slid neatly behind the wheel. The children squeezed in beside her as best as they could. Granny handed her big black purse to Elizabeth Anne. She settled her hat firmly on her head and smoothed her gloves on her hands. The children quickly buckled on seat belts as she reached for the stick shift.

"Hold on!" Granny yelled as the motor roared. It settled into a steady rumble. The pickup lurched once as Granny backed out of the parking space. She eased into the line of moving traffic.

Jimmy hung his head out the window and licked the air. "Salt air," he yelled.

Paul yanked him back. "Sit still, Jimmy. Don't bother Granny."

"He's not bothering me, Paul," Granny shouted. "This truck of Hiram's could find its own way home on a dark night!"

Jimmy looked at Paul.

"She means they drive this way a lot," Paul said. "Hold on."

The three children braced themselves for the ride across the causeway. On the other side was the island where Land's End had been built. They rumbled along, close to the speed limit, without meeting many cars. After a while the children got used to the noise of the old truck. They began to look around.

"Look, Gran," Elizabeth Anne said. "A T-Shirt Shop! That's new, isn't it?"

"So's that," Granny said, sniffing. She pointed to an area on the right.

They were passing the public beach. Pelicans covered the breakwater below Fisherman's Restaurant. The children were puzzled for a moment, wondering what she meant. The pelicans had always been there, hunting handouts. Then, down past the restaurant, the children saw brightly painted sheds and wheels.

"An amusement park!" Jimmy shouted. "Can we stop? Can we?"

"No, siree," Granny said. She shifted gears and turned down the road that ran alongside the beach. "Tourist trap! Nothing but a tourist trap!"

The children looked back wistfully. The bright colors were hidden by the green fronds of palms. They sighed in unison. Granny glanced at them. "Well, maybe," she said. "But I'm not promising!"

"Thanks, Gran," they replied. They watched the road eagerly as the houses grew fewer. For a while they could see nothing but sea grape, crape myrtle, and sea oats. Then they saw the cluster of palms and live oaks that surrounded the house called Land's End.

"Here it is," Elizabeth Anne said. She leaned against the seat belt to see better.

The house was old, but it was neat and freshly painted. Wide steps led past the latticed ground floor to the front porch that overlooked the ocean. Its two stories reached almost to the top of the live oaks. On the roof was a neat widow's walk.

Granny slowed down to turn into a driveway made of crushed shells and then stepped on the gas. Shells spattered from under the tires. An old man was watering the flowers beside the lattice. He jumped back wildly and dropped the hose.

"Now look at that," Granny muttered.

She stopped the truck and called to Hiram. "You know better than that," she called. "You've been here twenty years and I haven't run over you yet!"

He looked at her blankly. Then he cupped his hand behind his left ear. "What?"

Granny stopped the motor. "That man!" she said. "I don't know why I keep him on!"

She stepped down onto the driveway, still talking to herself. Elizabeth Anne and Paul grinned at each other. Even Granny knew that Hiram was teasing her, but she enjoyed the joke as much as he did.

The caretaker hugged the children in turn. His eyes were sparkling underneath the white eyebrows. "I got her that time, didn't I?"

"Hiram!" Elizabeth Anne grinned. "You shouldn't tease Granny!"

"A body has to have some fun," Hiram said. "Now you three are here, your Granny can have some peace. Run and stow your gear now. I'll see you later."

Elizabeth Anne said quickly, "I got dibs on the front bedroom!"

The children charged into the house. They raced into a wide hall and up a flight of waxed stairs. Elizabeth Anne was first to the top, and she took the larger room on the left.

Jimmy followed Paul into the one on the right. He dumped his things on the bed and went to the window. Down below, he saw Hiram on the beach path. Beside him, Jimmy saw a gleam of black.

"Blackie!" he yelled. He leaped across the bed and charged across the room. A minute later the front door slammed behind him, and he was running down the path to the beach.

Chapter Two
A Ball of Clay

Jimmy caught up with Hiram at the end of the path. Blackie heard the whisper of sand kicked up by Jimmy's sneakers. He turned and stood still for a moment. Then his tail began to wag.

"Blackie!" Jimmy said happily.

The black dog broke into a run. He leaped up on Jimmy and licked his face. The two fell down in the sand together, rolling over. Then Jimmy jumped up and ran down the beach with Blackie at his side.

The old man watched them run through the foam at the water's edge. At last he called them back. Jimmy and Blackie raced toward him. Jimmy stopped on the other side of Hiram to avoid the spray of water as Blackie shook himself.

"Git, dog," Hiram said. "Shoo!"

He turned to Jimmy, his eyes twinkling. "I see you haven't changed any."

Jimmy was crestfallen. "I haven't? Granny said Elizabeth Anne turned into a lady. And Paul is at least three inches taller than last year. And I did too change. I lost my front teeth, see?"

"I see," Hiram said. "Just don't be in such a hurry to grow up. You'll end up like Old Black Jack."

"Who was he? What happened to him? Was he a pirate?" Jimmy asked eagerly.

"Well," Hiram said happily, "you could say so. Not that it did him any good. Why, once he—" Hiram stopped. "Later, later. You run along now, son. I have work to do for your Granny."

"Tonight, Hiram?" Jimmy pleaded. "Will you tell us a story tonight?"

"Reckon so," Hiram agreed. "I've got a tale that's been just itching to be told. If it's all right with your Granny. Now run along."

But Hiram's tale didn't get told. By late afternoon the sky had turned a scuddy gray. Down on the beach, whitecaps raced the seagulls to land, and the pelicans huddled on the rocks. Hiram was busy making sure everything was tied down and safe before the storm broke.

The children stayed with Granny. They went from room to room in the darkening house to watch the approaching storm. Granny brought out flashlights and candles and hurricane lamps.

"Is it a real hurricane, Granny?" Jimmy asked. "Is it?"

"No, Jimmy," Granny answered. "It's just a blow this time, like Hiram says."

"Then can we go up on the widow's walk and watch the waves?" he asked.

Granny hesitated. "Well, all right. For a little while. I'll go with you."

On the top floor was a tiny stairway. Granny took an old key out of her apron pocket. She put it into the lock and turned it.

"The lock's getting rusty," she said. "Remind me to get Hiram to oil it."

"Okay," Jimmy replied.

He followed her onto the widow's walk. The wind whipped at their clothing and stung their eyes.

"Whew," Granny said. "We can't stay up here long!"

"Look, Granny," Jimmy said, pointing to the beach. "There's Hiram! And Blackie!"

Granny gave a startled cry. "Why, Hiram's going down to that amusement park! Whatever would he be doing down there?"

"He's after Blackie!" Jimmy leaned over the rail to see better.

Granny caught at him. "Don't lean so far over. Blackie will be all right. That dog is always up at the amusement park, chasing squirrels!"

"There, Blackie heard him. He's coming back," Jimmy said. "Look, Hiram's bringing him home."

They watched for a minute as the old man and the dog struggled against the wind. Then

Granny looked out at the sea. A wall of rain swept toward them.

"He'll just make it to his apartment over the garage if he hurries," she said. "Come, Jimmy. Let's go down."

They locked the door carefully and went below. Paul and Elizabeth Anne were in the kitchen. Since the lights had gone off, the kitchen was lit by three lamps. The warm glow made the kitchen feel like a safe haven against the storm. Even the rain that had begun to slam against the windows only made the kitchen seem cozier and safer.

They ate supper by lamplight. After the table was cleared, Granny brought her big Bible to the kitchen table. Jimmy looked at it in awe. It always surprised him that the Bible was as big as he remembered.

"What are we working on this summer?" he blurted out.

Granny raised her eyebrows. "Working on?"

"Mama always says we learn char—char—" He stumbled, trying to remember the word.

"Character," Elizabeth Anne said firmly.

"Yeah. Character." Jimmy rolled the syllables around his tongue. "We learn character every summer."

Granny smiled. "Well, we'll see."

The children listened as she read. Her clear, light voice seemed to push back the noise of the storm. Jimmy sat very still. Before the time for devotions was over, his eyelids began to close. No matter how hard he tried, he couldn't keep them open. His head slid down against Elizabeth Anne's arm. He didn't open his eyes again.

The next morning the storm had passed. Granny and the children went down to the beach. They carried baskets to collect the wreckage that the storm had washed ashore.

"We're the first ones out," Elizabeth Anne said. "It's like we're all alone in the world."

Jimmy shook his head. "Uh-uh, Hiram beat us. Look!"

Hiram and Blackie were down close to the amusement park. Jimmy watched as Hiram bent over and picked something up.

"Can I go with Hiram?" he asked.

"Just meet us back at the house for breakfast," Granny said. "Your tummy will tell you when it's time."

Jimmy whooped and ran down the beach. Blackie met him and they both trotted back to Hiram. Hiram showed him where to find big conch shells, starfish, and pale jellyfish. Jimmy sorted through barnacled driftwood, bits of chain, and scraps of fishing nets in search of a different kind of treasure. Soon his basket was full.

Everyone went to Land's End to clean his catch. Some of it was put outside to dry and be cured. Some could be taken upstairs right away. Jimmy arranged his shells carefully on the bookshelf by his bed. What I need is one big shell, he thought, like the one Hiram found. I'll look after breakfast.

After he had eaten, he went back to the beach. Blackie was down on the far end again. He ran toward Jimmy with something in his mouth.

"Hey, boy," Jimmy called. "Bring it here!"

Blackie sat down in front of Jimmy. He dropped a brown ball on the sand and wagged his tail.

Jimmy picked up the ball. "A clay ball? Where did you find that?" he asked.

Blackie only wagged his tail.

"Want to play catch, huh?" Jimmy said, picking up the ball. "Okay, I guess a clay ball is as good as any other. Come on, Blackie."

He and Blackie ran back and forth on the smooth, wet sand. Jimmy threw the ball, and Blackie caught it. He brought it back to Jimmy again and again.

The last time he brought it back, the ball was cracked. "Uh-oh, guess you chomped down too hard that time," Jimmy said.

He picked at the ball. A clump of clay came loose. "Hey, there's a rock in this," Jimmy said. "Who would put a rock in clay?"

He pried the rock out. It was green and it glittered, even through the dried smears of clay. "It's not a rock," Jimmy whispered. He turned it over and over. "It's a jewel!"

Chapter Three
A Pirate's Tale

Jimmy raced for the house with Blackie at his heels. His shouts brought Granny to the porch. Paul and Elizabeth Anne were right behind her. Even Hiram hurried across the stretch of green lawn, still holding his pruning shears.

"What is it, child?" Granny said anxiously. "Are you hurt?"

Jimmy shook his head, too out of breath to answer. He could only hold out his hand.

They looked at the ball blankly. "Clay?"

"No," Jimmy got out. "It's a jewel!"

He turned the clay. Sunlight glittered off the half-hidden jewel. Granny blinked. She took it from him and held it up to the light. The others exclaimed in wonder as it shimmered with green fire.

"An emerald, Hiram?" Granny said in amazement.

The old man peered at it. "Huh," he said slowly. A grin spread over his wrinkled face. "I'll be a yellow-backed horned toad if that's not part of Old Pegleg's treasure!"

"Pegleg? Treasure?" Four pairs of eyes focused on him.

"Is there more?"

"Was he a pirate?"

"I never heard of him!"

Granny frowned at Hiram. "No one ever proved that a pirate was in these waters. Hiram, if this is one of your stories. . . ."

"No, ma'am," Hiram replied indignantly. "I don't make up stories—" He stopped under Granny's stern look and then plunged on, "I just embroider them, sometimes."

"Just let us know which ones are needlework stories, then," Granny warned.

Hiram looked at her and then replied huffily, "Yes, ma'am."

"Pegleg, Hiram!" Jimmy said, tugging at Hiram's sleeve. "Tell us about Pegleg."

The sparkle came back to Hiram's eyes. He cleared his throat and looked toward the porch.

"All right, all right," Granny said sighing. "Come on up."

Hiram settled himself in the old wicker rocker. The children gathered around. Granny went into the house to get some lemonade. She gave Hiram a warning look as she passed. "Don't fill these children's heads with nonsense!"

"Yes, ma'am," he said meekly. But before she came back he was well into his story.

"It was many, many years ago. Old Man Winter was whipping the waves and sending them crashing onto the beach so's a body had to shout to hear himself speak. My granddaddy was walking along the high road, up there, heading for home and a warm bed. It was nigh dark, for Granddad had been working late at the shipyard in the harbor. He said he never knew what made him look down at the beach, but he did. There was a small boat pulled up out of the waves, with its sail still dangling."

"Was it wrecked?"

"Didn't look like it to Granddad. But it looked odd to him, that late in the day. So he went closer, just to see."

"What? What?"

"All he saw was the boat. That, and a chest. A wee one, but it was bolted and locked like it held all the treasure in the world."

"Did it have jewels? Did it have pieces of eight?" Jimmy asked eagerly.

"Well, I don't rightly know. Granddad crept across the sand, keeping a sharp eye out for any strangers, y'see. He reached the chest without seeing one soul. But just as he reached down to touch it, BAM!" Hiram slapped his hands together.

"What?" Elizabeth Anne squealed.

"Somebody banged him on the back of the head with something heavy. Something like a shovel," Hiram said meaningfully.

"You mean the pirate was there? He was ready to bury the chest?" Jimmy asked. "And he hit your grandfather?"

"Yep," Hiram said. "That's just what Granddad thought when he came to."

"Well, was it?"

"Never found out," Hiram said. "Nothing was there. No boat, no chest, no pirate. But Granddad knew what had happened to him."

"Sure he didn't trip over his own feet?" Granny asked.

"Now that's the attitude everybody took," Hiram complained. "But that didn't stop Granddad. Because he saw the tracks leading up the beach, right there!"

He turned to point in the direction of the amusement park. Jimmy shivered with excitement.

"And those tracks were one foot, one circle, one foot, one circle, all the way!"

"A peg leg," Jimmy said.

"A peg leg," Hiram agreed.

"But didn't the tracks lead to the treasure chest?" Paul asked, puzzled.

"Well, they did, son," Hiram said. "But not right to it. The waves had washed most of the tracks away. And by the time Granddad came back the next morning, the trail was lost in the turn of the tide."

"And no one ever found the treasure?" Elizabeth Anne was wide-eyed.

"Not even Granddad," Hiram said. "Though it wasn't from lack of looking."

"It certainly wasn't," Granny said with disapproval. "He spent the rest of his days wandering the beach with a shovel. He dug great holes everywhere, but not a speck of silver did he find!"

Jimmy didn't hear her. He was lost in thought. "A real pirate! Right here on our beach!"

"Well, now, Jimmy," Hiram said hastily. "It was just like your Granny said. Nobody ever got the right or wrong of it. The boat was only seen that one night and then never again in all the history of Pelican Cove."

Jimmy looked at the emerald. "But this proves it," he said. "Pegleg really was here!"

"But why is the emerald wrapped in clay?" Paul leaned over to look again. "Why wasn't it in the chest?"

"I don't know," Hiram said thoughtfully. "Maybe Pegleg was afraid to leave the chest because he had been seen."

"Maybe he just emptied part of it into a hiding place," Paul suggested.

Excitement grew in Hiram's voice. "Yes. Yes, I remember hearing about pirate's caches where small jewels were wrapped in clay and hidden in out-of-the-way places!"

"Then Pegleg's treasure may not have been buried on the beach," Paul said, disgusted. "It could be anywhere."

"No." Hiram's eyes were glowing. "Not anywhere. Granddad was only knocked out for a couple of hours. It has to be close. Very close."

"And we're going to find it," Jimmy shouted. "We're going to find the treasure!"

Chapter Four

Spades and Shovels

"Can we, Granny?" Elizabeth Anne asked.

Paul and Jimmy watched her hopefully.

"Why anyone would spend his summer running around after something that isn't there is beyond me," she said.

Jimmy drooped. "Aw, Granny."

"Just think," Paul pleaded. "What an adventure this could be! Buried treasure! What if we find it?"

Granny sighed. "I can see you've got treasure-hunting fever. Sometimes it's best to let it run its course. Hiram, see that they have good equipment. I don't want them to hurt themselves."

"Thanks, Gran!" The thanks came from all three, with an extra hug thrown in from Elizabeth Anne. Then they disappeared toward the storage shed before Granny could change her mind.

"Hiram," Granny said sternly. "I'm holding you responsible for those children."

"Yes'm," Hiram said meekly. "I'll see they come to no harm."

She watched as he hurried around the corner of the house. Then she took the gem inside to clean it up.

Armed with shovels and spades, Hiram and the children went down the path to the beach. Blackie scampered ahead of them.

"Which way do we go, Hiram?" Jimmy asked eagerly.

"Grandad said Pegleg's tracks went this way," Hiram answered. He led the way along the beach. "After that, who knows?"

"I think we should try up on the dunes," Paul suggested. "Maybe he took them up there."

Elizabeth Anne objected. "It's too hot up there. Let's stay down on the beach."

"I bet there's a cave out on the point," Jimmy said. He turned back the other way. "I'm going to go find it."

"There's no cave there," Paul said sharply. "There never has been."

"How do you know?" Jimmy said.

"Whoa, boys," Hiram said. "Paul is right, Jimmy. There are no caves along this stretch of beach. That's why we always thought the treasure was buried in the sand. I think Paul probably had the right idea. Let's head for the road."

Elizabeth Anne groaned, but she followed the old man and the boys. They picked their way through the sliding sand until they reached the upper road. Here, shell and rock were mixed with the packed sand and made the going easier.

"Why don't we just stay on the road?" Elizabeth Anne said hopefully.

"That wouldn't do any good," Paul replied. "This road has been worked on over the years.

If anything had been hidden here, it would have been found long ago. Right, Hiram?"

"Right." Hiram stopped to look for Jimmy. "Hey, Jimmy," he called. "Come down from there!"

Jimmy had chased Blackie up to the top of one of the dunes. Blackie ran ahead of him and disappeared over the ridge.

"But Blackie went over there," Jimmy called back.

"Let him go," Hiram said. "He'll come back when he's ready. That's part of his regular route."

Jimmy gave Blackie a longing look. Then he slid back down. "Regular route?"

"Other dogs have back yards as their territory. The beach is Blackie's. He makes his run every day—down past the amusement park, over to the river, then back to the point. That's his territory."

"Then that's where the jewels are," Jimmy said.

"What?" Elizabeth Anne gave him a puzzled look.

"He's right," Hiram said, his eyes gleaming. "Blackie brought him the ball, y'see. Blackie got the ball in his territory."

"So where do we start digging?" Paul asked.

Hiram scratched his head. "I just don't know. Granddad covered the beach pretty well. I've done some digging myself. So I know where it isn't. Maybe we've been a little hasty about digging. Maybe we ought to go back to the house and draw a map of Blackie's territory."

"We could mark it off in quadrants and search them one by one," Paul suggested.

"Hydrants?"

"No, quadrants, Jimmy," Paul explained. "Sort of like squares. We'll do one square at a time."

"Good idea, Paul," Hiram agreed. "I have graph paper and pens at my place."

They started back to the garage. Jimmy followed, but he kept looking back for Blackie. The dog was nowhere to be seen.

He gave up and clattered up the stairs after the others. He stopped at the open door of Hiram's apartment. Like his brother and sister, he had never been in the apartment. Granny had insisted that Hiram have one place where he could not be disturbed.

Jimmy looked about in awe. A brisk breeze from the ocean fanned the curtains at the big windows. Bookshelves lined the walls under the windows. They were stuffed with books. Books were stacked on end tables, on counters, and on the dining room table. Maps lined the walls. And from the ceiling hung shells, perfect shells.

On one side of the room was a huge salt water tank. Jimmy made a beeline for it. He forgot all about the treasure as he hung over the tank. Hermit crabs scuttled along the bottom. A sea anemone swayed lazily in the water. Coral made hiding places for angelfish and sunfish. Jimmy was poking at a snail when Elizabeth Anne called him.

She and Paul were bending over the maps that Hiram had spread on the table. "Look, Jimmy," she called. "This is Pelican Cove."

Hiram made dots at the points that he thought marked the boundaries of Blackie's territory. Then he connected the dots. Jimmy laughed.

"Dot to dot," he said.

"Yep," Hiram agreed. He divided the area into four parts. "Now we have it. You understand that this is just guesswork, don't you? Blackie may go farther than this."

"I hope not," Paul said. "This is a lot to cover."

"Well, let's go," Jimmy said. "I want to find a red jewel. We can give it to Mom for her birthday. Besides, I want to find Blackie."

He was out the door and down the steps before Hiram could fold up the map. Elizabeth Anne yelled for him to wait, and then she threw up her hands.

"We'll catch up with him," Hiram said. "We can see him all the way down the beach."

They started searching in the first quadrant. Hiram made them promise not to disturb anything. "Put it back the way you found it," he said. "Folks got sort of put out at Granddad's holes."

"Put out?" Jimmy asked from behind them.

"Mad," Paul grunted. He shoveled sand faster. "I don't think that's a problem. This hole keeps filling up as fast as I make it," he said.

"Yeah," Elizabeth Anne agreed. She quit shoveling. "Didn't pirates mark the spot or something?"

"Good idea," Hiram said. "What would make a good landmark? Remember, it has to have been around for a long time."

"The palms in Quadrant 1," Paul suggested. "They make a funny pattern."

"Or the rocky ledge over there by the road in Quadrant 3," Elizabeth Anne said.

"You know," Hiram said thoughtfully. "Your Granny may have a few ideas herself. She was born right here at Land's End. She'll know what changes have been made over the years, maybe even better than I do."

"Yeah. And she still has that pitcher of lemonade," Jimmy said. "Last one up is a rotten egg!"

He dropped his spade and ran. When the others reached the front porch, Jimmy was coming back outside.

"I can't find her," he said.

"What?" Elizabeth Anne stopped, gasping for breath.

"Granny's gone," Jimmy said. "And so is the emerald!"

Chapter Five

Treasure Fever

"Where could she be?" Elizabeth Anne asked. "It's not like Gran to leave without saying a word to us."

"Now, hold on," Hiram said. "She probably went to the grocery store to pick up something she needed for supper. She wouldn't want to come all the way down to the beach to tell us that. Not if she's coming right back."

"The pickup's gone," Paul called. "Hiram's probably right. She must have gone to the store."

No one wanted to leave the porch. They sat down and waited, watching the road to the house. At last they heard the roar of the pickup.

"It's Gran!" Elizabeth Anne took off running. But Jimmy beat her to the pickup.

"Granny! Where've you been?" he demanded.

"Down to the museum, talking to Mr. Culpepper," she replied.

Hiram groaned. "Not Mr. Culpepper? Old busybody Culpepper?"

Granny frowned slightly at his tone. She pulled off her gloves and took the pin out of her straw hat. "Mr. Culpepper is the curator of the museum, you know. You just can't pick up gems on the beach and walk off with them."

"You can't?" Even Hiram looked crestfallen.

"No," Granny added, "but there is a finder's fee. A good one."

"Then we can still look for the treasure?" Jimmy persisted.

"If that's what you want," Granny replied. "But I have to warn you. Hiram is right about Mr. Culpepper. By noon tomorrow you will have all the help you will ever need."

"What do you mean, Gran?" Elizabeth Anne asked.

"Cyrus Culpepper is not known for keeping secrets. Tomorrow, everybody in town will know about the emerald Jimmy found. And everybody will want to help you find the rest of the treasure."

"They can't." Jimmy's eyebrows came together in a dark frown. "We found it first."

"We sure did." Elizabeth Anne was annoyed. "Why should they get in on it?"

Gran was quiet for a minute. Then she said, "You found the emerald. And if there really are any more jewels, whoever finds them will get a finder's fee, just as you did for the emerald."

"Then let's get going," Paul said. "Maybe we can find the rest of the treasure before it gets dark."

They went back to work. Even Elizabeth Anne shoveled with all her might. And Jimmy left Blackie to play alone while he dug with his spade. But by supper time, all they had were tired muscles and big appetites.

They ate everything on their plates and asked for more. Granny bustled about the kitchen. "Guess this nonsense has some good in it," she said cheerfully. "Growing children need good food."

After devotions all three children were ready for bed. Granny shooed them upstairs before dark. No one protested.

The next morning Jimmy was the first one up. He stumbled to the window. Rubbing still-sleepy eyes, he started to call for Blackie.

The shout stuck in his throat. The beach was full of holes! They made a jagged line down the beach. Jimmy blinked. When he opened his eyes, the holes were still there. And there were people farther down the beach—people with shovels.

"Paul," Jimmy called. He shook his brother. "Wake up! There are people down there!"

"People?" Paul murmured sleepily. "What people?"

He rolled over and went back to sleep. Jimmy shook him again. "Treasure hunters!"

Paul was on his feet before Jimmy finished. He stuck his head out the window. "Oh, no," he moaned. "Jimmy, go get Elizabeth Anne."

All three children were dressed and out the door before Granny could call them for breakfast. Arms folded, she stood on the porch and watched them go. Then she shook out her apron and went back inside.

Hiram was already on the beach. Blackie frisked around him. He wanted to play, but no one was interested. Not even Jimmy. The beach was filled with working people.

"That must be Mr. Culpepper over there," Paul said. "I guess you were right, Hiram."

"Yep," Hiram said. He tossed out another shovel of sand and wiped his brow. "And there is Miss Abbott from the library."

Elizabeth Anne turned around. A thin woman trotted through the sand toward them. Dark glasses covered her eyes, and a large straw hat shaded her from the sun.

"Hello there," she called. "Isn't this wonderful? A pirate on our beach! Why, Hiram, all these years we thought—" She stopped and put her hand to her throat.

"That my granddad had lost his marbles," Hiram finished for her.

"We didn't find any marbles. We found a clay ball," Jimmy said.

Paul turned to explain, but Jimmy was already chasing Blackie down the beach.

"Well, in any case," Miss Abbott said kindly, "we were certainly wrong, weren't we?"

"Appears so," Hiram said, looking at the growing crowd on the beach.

Jimmy came racing back up with Blackie. "Hey," he called. "Someone's got a bulldozer up there."

"A bulldozer!" Hiram dropped his shovel. "Jimmy, run tell your Granny to call the mayor. I'll put a stop to this!"

Granny and Mayor Tidwell arrived about half an hour later. They found Hiram facing down a large, beefy-looking man. They were standing in front of a bulldozer. The man had his hands on his hips. He looked hot and angry.

Jimmy ran to Granny. "Better hurry, Granny," he said. "Hiram's getting awful mad."

Granny smiled. "It looks like he has company."

"Company?"

"I mean both of them look angry," Granny explained.

"Oh," Jimmy said. He and Blackie followed them to the crowd that had gathered around the bulldozer.

"Hold on," said the mayor. "What's going on here?"

He shook his head at the clamor of explanations. "One at a time," he said. "You, Hiram. You go first."

Hiram explained as quickly as he could. The onlookers murmured with excitement as he told about the clay ball.

"I heard it was washed up by the storm," shouted one digger, "and that hundreds were lying on the beach just waiting for someone to pick them up."

"I heard that the boy here found a whole chest of gold coins," called another.

"And that at least two more chests were buried under the sand," a bearded man said. "So where are they?"

"Move out of my way," said the large man. "I'll unearth any chests hidden here in a matter of minutes."

"Don't be hasty, Jake," the mayor said. He frowned at the crowd. "Or any of you. You could wreck this coastline before the day's out."

"Then what'll we do?" shouted a woman.

"We'll wait," the mayor said firmly. "This beach is off-limits to everybody! And I mean everybody!"

"For how long?" The man's tone was ugly. "Long enough for you to get the treasure yourself?"

"The beach will be patrolled by the volunteer police department until we decide what to do," the mayor replied. He turned to the crowd. "Town meeting. Tonight in City Hall. Be there."

The people began to pick up their gear. A man made his way through the crowd to the bulldozer.

"We have a quick job, Jake," he called. "The storm washed out part of the beach near the amusement park. Tumbled down that old refreshment stand. They'll give us a flat one hundred for finishing the job."

"Not now," Jake growled. "I'm parking this 'dozer up on the road where I can see what's going on here."

"But—"

"I said it'll wait," Jake said.

Jimmy watched as the man hurried back up the path to the road. The bulldozer roared up behind him. Jake parked it where he had a good view of the beach.

"Wow, Blackie," Jimmy whispered. He rubbed the dog's head. "I think we'll stay out of his way—right, boy?"

Blackie looked up at Jimmy and barked.

Chapter Six

Dark Shadows

That afternoon Elizabeth Anne went down to the kitchen to help Granny bake. Hiram had work to do, and Paul wanted to help him. Jimmy went up to his room to play. After a while the billowing curtains drew him to the window.

He leaned on the windowsill and rested his head on his arms. He watched the waves roll toward the shore and crash onto the sand. The foam fanned out onto the sand like white lace.

It spilled over into the holes in the sand. The foam slipped away and left small pools of water. Blackie trotted down from the house. He stopped to sniff at one of the pools. He barked sharply, backed up, and shook his head.

Jimmy laughed. He leaned farther out the window. "Gotcha, Blackie," he yelled. "What was it, a crab?"

Blackie looked up at the window and barked again. He trotted back and forth, whimpering.

"I'm coming," Jimmy called.

He went across the bed in one stride. Halfway down the stairs, he remembered that the beach was off-limits. He headed for the kitchen. Granny and Elizabeth Anne were baking cookies. Jimmy took one and stuffed it into his mouth.

"Good," he mumbled and turned back for two more.

"That's all, son," Granny said. "Supper will come soon enough."

"Blackie's out on the beach, Granny," Jimmy said. "May I go get him?"

"Don't talk with your mouth full, Jimmy," Elizabeth Anne said.

Granny brushed back a stray strand of hair. She tucked it back into the neat braids that wound around her head. "I think that would be fine, Jimmy," she said. "The beach isn't closed for regular use—just digging. Go play with Blackie."

Jimmy was gone before she finished. He half ran, half slid down the path to the beach. Blackie met him at the bottom. Jimmy followed him back to the hole. He lay down and probed in the water.

A crab scuttled up one side of the hole. It walked sideways across the sand, chased by the barking dog. Jimmy let the water settle and looked again. A starfish clung to a rock in the bottom.

Jimmy pulled it out of a tangle of seaweed and let it crawl along his arm. Its suckers felt clammy on his skin. He let the starfish drop off into the water.

"I'll bet these holes are full of stuff," Jimmy said eagerly. "Let's check them out, Blackie."

He was at the third hole when Blackie began to whine. He trotted away from the hole to stand between Jimmy and the sand dunes.

"What's the matter, Blackie?" Jimmy asked. He looked toward the dunes. A shadow swept across one dune. Jimmy frowned. He glanced up in the sky, but no bird circled overhead.

"Is anyone there?" Jimmy called.

There was no answer. Suddenly Blackie began to bark furiously. Jimmy grabbed for the dog. He shivered.

"Let's go back home," he said.

Blackie didn't protest. He trotted beside Jimmy, wagging his tail. When they reached the house, Blackie lay down on the porch. Jimmy went inside to find the others.

He told Granny about the shadow.

"There was somebody watching me," he said. "I just know there was."

"I've lived on this island all my life," Granny said slowly. "I know every man, woman, and child by name. No one here would hurt you."

Elizabeth Anne put down her bowl. "Everything has changed, Gran," she said. "Hunting for treasure isn't fun any more."

"Do you want to give it up?" Granny asked.

"Not yet," Elizabeth Anne admitted. "But I wish everything was back the way it used to be."

"Perhaps it will be," Granny said. "We'll get some things straightened out at the meeting tonight."

But the meeting didn't turn out the way Granny had expected. Miss Abbott was on the town council. So were Cullen Ludlow, Ramon Corez, and Tom Hadmore. Every one of them had been digging on the beach.

The speeches were long and loud. In the end, the council voted to divide the beach up into sections and to allow only hand-digging.

Granny stood up when the markers were passed around for drawing lots. "I'll have none of this," she said. "Hiram, you can stay if you want, but I'm taking the children home."

"I'm with you," Hiram said. "Granddad's treasure is beginning to have a bitter taste."

Jimmy looked at Hiram. "Like a drink all shook up and gone flat," he said.

Hiram gave him a surprised look. "Right, Jimmy," he said. "Just like that."

That night during devotions Granny read the story from the Bible that told about Rachel's taking her father's household idols. Jimmy listened hard to what Granny was saying about greed. But he didn't understand what Rachel's idols had to do with what was happening on the beach.

The next morning they sat on the porch and watched the council members divide the beach into sections. Each section had a number. People lined the road along the beach. They were burdened down with all kinds of digging tools. They carried water jugs and umbrellas. And each person held a numbered card that would match a numbered lot.

"Looks just like a gold field," Hiram said. "Watch, now, you're about to see a gold rush!"

When the signal was given, the people poured over the dunes, each one heading for the section that matched his number. In a matter of minutes, sand was flying into the air.

Jimmy stared. Paul stalked back and forth. Elizabeth Anne moaned. "Oh, I wish Jimmy had never found that jewel. They're going to ruin our summer."

"Maybe not," Hiram said slowly. A chuckle began deep in his throat. "They are clearing those sections mighty fast. Look at Nat McDougall use that shovel! I never thought I would ever see that man work so hard."

Granny smiled. "It does look like good exercise," she said. "They'll all get some profit from it. After the sore muscles, that is."

And muscles were sore by late afternoon. The sections had been mostly cleared, too. Tired, discouraged people headed back up the sand dunes.

Only a few remained to argue. "If you had let me use my 'dozer, we'd have found something," Jake insisted.

The vacated holes attracted Blackie. The dog trotted down the path. He was nosing around Jake's section when one of Jake's workers saw him.

"Get that dog out of here!" he shouted. He ran toward Blackie, waving a shovel.

Jimmy launched himself off the porch. He headed down to Jake's section, screeching, "Don't you touch my dog!"

Hiram and Paul were right behind him. "Jimmy!" they yelled.

They caught up with him at the hole Jake had dug. Jimmy was holding Blackie by the collar and glaring up at Jake and the man who held the shovel. The man had a tanned face and stringy-looking, dark hair.

"Go on, kid," Jake said gruffly. "We won't hurt your dog."

"Hey, aren't you the kid that found the emerald?" the man with the shovel asked. His small, dark eyes gleamed.

Jimmy didn't answer. He backed away, still holding Blackie.

"Then that's the dog that brought it to you," Jake said thoughtfully. "Maybe we've been going about this all wrong. Maybe we need that dog. He'd lead us right to the treasure!"

"No, you don't," Jimmy said. His chin jutted out. "I'm taking Blackie home."

Jake pulled out a roll of money. "Here, kid," he said, peeling off twenty-dollar bills. "I'll buy the dog."

"No way," Jimmy said. His chin jutted out even farther. "Blackie's not for sale!"

Chapter Seven
Back in the Game

That night Blackie slept inside for the first time. He lay beside Jimmy's bed. Before Jimmy went to sleep, he leaned over to pat Blackie's head.

"Nobody's going to get you, Blackie," he said. "Don't you worry."

The dog licked Jimmy's hand. Then he curled up on the rug and gave a gusty sigh. In a few minutes they were both asleep, Jimmy's hand still touching the dog.

When dawn came, the dog yawned. He stood up and stretched. Then he padded out of the room and down the stairs.

Jimmy awoke later. He turned over to look for Blackie, but the dog was gone. Jimmy tossed back the covers and hurried downstairs. Granny was in the kitchen.

"Blackie's gone!" Jimmy said, near tears.

"Land sakes, son," Granny said. She comforted the boy. "He's used to getting up early in the morning. I let him out myself."

Jimmy opened the back door. He saw Blackie streaking across the lawn after a squirrel. The dog chased the squirrel up a tree. Then he sat at the foot of the tree. The squirrel chattered back at him from a safe distance.

"Blackie will be watching that tree for an hour." Granny spoke from behind Jimmy's shoulder. "Plenty of time for you to eat your breakfast."

"Why does he chase squirrels?" Jimmy asked.

"No cats around here," Granny replied. "The poor animal has to do something for exercise when you aren't here."

Jimmy grinned. "I'm sure glad you have Blackie. Elizabeth Anne helps you, and Paul helps Hiram. I take care of Blackie."

"That you do, son," Granny said. She wiped her hands on her apron. "Now, let's get those sleepyheads out of bed."

By the time everyone had dressed and appeared for breakfast, Granny was ready. The table was set for five. Pancakes and eggs and bacon brought them eagerly to the table. While eating, they made plans for the day.

"Are the diggers still out there?" Elizabeth Anne asked.

"Since before dawn," Granny replied. "Still hard at it."

"They're wasting their time," Hiram said chuckling.

"Why?" Paul asked. He set his glass of milk down carefully. "They might just find it."

"Nope." Hiram's eyes twinkled. "They won't. But Blackie might."

"How could Blackie—" Paul hesitated. "Oh, because of what Jake said yesterday?"

"Blackie found it," Jimmy agreed. "And he knows where it is."

"The problem," Hiram said, "is how to get him to tell us."

"We can follow him around," Elizabeth Anne suggested. "Sooner or later, he'll go back to the same spot."

"I think Jake has the same idea," Hiram said. "No, it has to look like no one is following him."

"So how can we follow him without following him?" Jimmy was puzzled.

"We can't, but you can," Hiram said.

The children looked at him in surprise.

"Jimmy has been playing with Blackie ever since he arrived," Hiram said. "Everybody around here has seen them playing in the summertime. They expect to see them together."

"True," Granny said dryly. "But what about Jimmy? Aren't you putting him into some danger?"

"Well," Hiram replied, "it's like you said. What real danger is there? But just in case, we can put a bug on him."

Jimmy's eyebrows shot up. "A bug? An electronic bug, like in detective stories?"

"Right, Jimmy," Hiram said, warming up to his subject. "Maybe we could use two. A locater on Blackie and a listening bug on you. Then if we lost one, we would have the other."

Granny tried not to laugh, but her eyes were twinkling. "Hiram," she said, "you're as bad as the children. You've been reading too many detective stories."

"Oh, Gran," Elizabeth Anne said. "It would be fun!"

"Yes, Granny, let us!" Paul and Jimmy were in complete agreement.

Granny threw up her hands. "All right," she said. "But if this gets out of hand, you have to stop. I have a responsibility to your parents."

"I'll be right with them," Hiram said solemnly. "Every step of the way."

"I'll bet you will," Granny said with amusement.

They drove in to Abbeville to get the equipment. The salesman at Electronics, Inc., helped them select just what they needed.

"These will do just fine," Hiram said. He pulled out his wallet. "What do I owe you?"

When the salesman quoted the price, Hiram whistled. "That's a lot of money for two tiny scraps of metal."

The salesman looked at the old man and the children. "Need it long?"

"About a week should do it," Hiram said.

"How about a rental?"

"Rental?"

"Sure." The salesman beamed. "Don't do much of a turnover in surveillance equipment. I'll rent the bugs to you for one week. Bring them back in good condition, and everything's A-Okay."

The smile returned to Hiram's face. "That's great," he said. "We'll do it!"

"You guys setting up a detective agency?" he asked, grinning at them.

Hiram shook his head. "Nothing like that," he replied. "Just a little fishing job."

"Well, you let me know what kind of fish you reel in with that baby," the salesman said. "Just bring them back in good condition if you expect a refund."

"Okay, kiddos." Hiram chuckled as they piled into the pickup. "We're back in the game!"

But when they reached Land's End, Granny met them on the porch.

"Blackie's gone," she called. "I can't find him anywhere!"

Jimmy was out of the truck as soon as it stopped. "Jake got him!"

Granny stopped him before he could charge down the beach. "Wait, Jimmy," she said. "We don't know that."

Jimmy's face was white under his freckles and his eyes were stormy. "You know he did. And I'll get him if he hurt Blackie!"

"Settle down, son," Hiram said. He stopped beside Jimmy. "Okay, we'll go look. Maybe he's down at the amusement park."

They went down the beach path in single file. When the walking was easier, they turned down the beach.

"See, Jimmy?" Hiram said. He pointed at tracks on the wet sand. "He went this way. He's probably on his rounds."

Elizabeth Anne ran ahead. "Hey, look!"

Jimmy ran to catch up with her. Near one of the holes, boot tracks merged with the paw prints. Beyond that, the paw prints walked alongside the boot tracks. They led back to the road.

Jimmy struggled up the dune. The others followed. At the top, the tracks ended. There was nothing. Not to the right. Not to the left. Just nothing.

"He's gone this time," Jimmy said tearfully. "Blackie's really gone!"

Chapter Eight

The Shack on Heron Creek

"Now that does it!" Granny's eyes snapped with anger. "Taking someone's pet! I've known Jake Lester's ma for nearly fifteen years. If anyone can get to the bottom of this, she can. Come on. We'll pay her a friendly visit."

Hiram's pickup crunched back down the shell road. Granny and Hiram sat in the front. Paul, Elizabeth Anne, and Jimmy sat in the back of the truck, braced against the cab.

"Don't worry, Jimmy," Elizabeth Anne said. "We'll find him."

Jimmy scrubbed hard at his still-wet face. "Yeah. Granny'll get him back."

The pickup turned onto the beach road. Jimmy was quiet the rest of the way to Frenchman's Inlet. He watched the trees and shrubs slide past on the left side of the truck. He didn't want to look down the beach where Blackie should have been.

Hiram turned down a dirt road and eased the truck up to a small house near the water. Mrs. Lester was sitting on the porch. She was rocking and fanning herself. She got up and waited for them to approach.

"Come, sit a spell," she said cheerfully. "I've been hoping for a bit of company. Rest yourselves."

Granny took the rocker next to her. Hiram sat on the porch rail. The children lined themselves up on the front steps. They waited expectantly for Granny to ask about Blackie.

Instead, Granny mentioned the storm. The two women fell into a discussion about the weather. The children stared in amazement. They wiggled on the hard steps.

Hiram glanced down at them, eyes twinkling. A slight shake of his head was enough to stop Elizabeth Anne and Paul. But not Jimmy.

Each of the children was introduced in turn. Granny left Jimmy for last. Mrs. Lester looked him over with shrewd eyes. "This one seems to have a problem," she said. "Has the look of my Jake when things don't go his way."

"Maybe," Granny said easily. She led the conversation away from Jimmy to the treasure hunters on the beach.

Red swept into Jimmy's face. He unclenched his fists and tried to sit still. Jake, he thought to himself—I don't look like Jake Lester!

"I hear your dog found an emerald," Mrs. Lester said. "Jake was telling me about it the other night. He took quite a liking to that dog."

"I'll bet," Jimmy muttered. Elizabeth Anne gave him a sharp nudge. Jimmy fell silent.

"I thought maybe he did," Granny said. "And we wanted to get his help. The silly dog's off somewhere and we can't find him. Do you think Jake could help?"

Jimmy felt his jaw drop open. He blinked. Granny was asking Jake to help find Blackie!

"If anybody can, it'll be my Jake," Mrs. Lester said. "He's a mite rough-mannered and all, but he loves animals. He'd not hurt a wee thing."

She got up and headed for the open door. "He'll be home in a few minutes. You just set right there and don't stir yourselves. I'll get you some of my banana-nut bread. Fresh baked this morning."

Jimmy was still licking crumbs and melted butter off his fingers when he looked up and saw Jake. The big man was striding up the path to the house. Jimmy froze. The plate slid out of his lap. It landed on the grass with a dull thud.

"Here he is now," Mrs. Lester said. "These folks came to see you, Jake."

Jake took off his hat when he saw Granny. "Ma'am." He nodded to the others. "What can I do for you?"

He stopped in front of Jimmy. The boy found himself staring at muddy boots and a length of faded denim. He started to rise. A swift pinch from Elizabeth Anne kept him rooted to the steps.

"These folks lost a dog," Mrs. Lester said. "They were hoping you might help find him."

Jake Lester glanced down at Jimmy. "You mean that old black dog? The one that found Pegleg's treasure?"

Jimmy nodded.

He shrank back as the big man knelt in front of him. "Hey, son," Jake said, "I lost a dog once. Roughest time I ever went through. Sure, I'll help you find your dog."

"But—I thought you took him," Jimmy blurted out.

Jake looked surprised. Then he laughed, a big laugh that began deep in his chest. When he finished, his face was redder than ever.

"I guess I did spout off a bit the other day," he said. "But it's not in my nature to hurt a dog."

"Not Jake," his mother agreed. "He'll find your dog for you, son."

"Maybe sooner than you think," Jake said thoughtfully. "I've got a good idea where to look. You folks can follow me in your truck."

A few minutes later, the two pickup trucks were bouncing along the river road. About five miles out, they came to a weather-beaten old house. Jake pulled into the yard. Hiram stopped behind him.

The sound of the trucks started a frenzy of barking. Jimmy looked around eagerly, but he couldn't see any dogs. He leaped over the side and started toward the sound.

Jake walked back to the truck. He stopped Jimmy. "Wait here," he said.

Granny told Jimmy to get back into the truck. Jimmy obeyed reluctantly. Then all three children stood up so that they could see over the cab of the truck. They watched as Jake strode up to the sagging porch. The door opened and a man stepped out.

"Hey," Jimmy whispered, "it's the man who chased Blackie!"

The stringy-haired man glanced toward the truck. His dark eyes narrowed. He looked back at Jake and leaned against a crooked porch post.

The children couldn't hear what Jake said. They didn't have to. They could tell from the way he moved that he was angry. The other man answered him sullenly. They talked for a few minutes. Then they went around the side of the house.

The barking quieted and then became louder. Jimmy held his breath. Suddenly Blackie came charging around the building. Jimmy met him halfway.

The others piled out of the truck. They hurried to pet Blackie. The dog frisked around happily. Jake and the other man came back around the building and up onto the rickety porch. After Jake said something else to him, the man stomped through the doorway, kicking the door shut behind him.

Jake left the porch and hurried down to join the others. "The dog's been well cared for," he said. "And I fired Bill. I hired him off the

mainland when I was short-handed. Should've known better. But if you want to press charges—"

Granny shook her head. "No," she said firmly. She shook Jake's hand. "We got what we came for. Thanks to you, Jake."

"You're welcome, ma'am," Jake said gruffly. "Now maybe we ought to get going. Bill's just squatting on this property. He'll be lighting out now."

Hiram hustled them into the truck and backed out. All the way home, the children sang at the top of their lungs.

When they reached Land's End, Jimmy stopped beside Granny. "Thanks, Granny," he said. "You were great!"

Her eyes twinkled. "Well, I guess I did keep you from accusing someone wrongly. It's best not to be hasty."

Jimmy gave her an embarrassed look. "Yes, ma'am. I'll get the facts first next time."

"Just remember, the folks on this island may have a touch of treasure fever, but they are still our friends," Granny said. "Treat them as such. The fever will go; the friends will remain."

"Then it's all right to go back to our search?" Elizabeth Anne asked.

"Fine, but—" Granny hesitated. "It won't hurt to take precautions. I trust our friends. I don't trust any man who would take a dog."

Chapter Nine
Tailing a Dog

"Hey," Jimmy squeaked. "You stuck me!"

"Well, be still," Elizabeth Anne said. She blew her hair out of her eyes and got ready to try again. Jimmy wriggled away.

"Let me try," Granny said. She took the tiny bit of metal gently. "Stand still, Jimmy. Where would be the safest place to put this?"

Hiram was securing the other bug to Blackie's collar. He looked up. "Make sure it won't get wet. I've got to return these in good shape."

"In the pocket?" Granny asked.

"Fine," Hiram replied.

Granny pinned the bug inside Jimmy's pocket and zipped the pocket. "Jimmy," she said, "you keep that pocket zipped, okay?"

Jimmy nodded. "Can we go yet?"

Granny checked his pocket. "I guess so."

They all went to the porch to watch Jimmy and Blackie head down the path to the beach. Blackie trotted ahead eagerly, glad to be free again. Jimmy followed. Every few steps he hunched his shoulder up to his head.

"What's he doing?" Elizabeth Anne asked. "What's he doing?"

Paul began to laugh. "He's trying to talk into the bug. If he keeps this up, he'll be thrown off the beach."

Even Granny chuckled at Jimmy's odd movements. "Well, I guess we'd better go see what he's saying," she said.

They gathered around the receiver Hiram had set up in the living room. Hiram adjusted the dials. Jimmy's voice was coming in clearly.

"We're turning down the beach," he whispered hoarsely. "We just passed Talmadge Duncan's plot."

Suddenly Jimmy switched back to his normal voice. "Hi, Talmadge, what'cha found?"

"Hi, Jimmy," Talmadge replied. "Got chiggers, huh?"

"Chiggers?" Jimmy sounded puzzled.

"Yeah, I saw you trying to rub your shoulder with your head. Funniest way to scratch I've ever seen. Won't do any good anyhow. Those little bugs burrow in and you just can't get rid of them."

"Oh."

"Try kerosene. Worked for me."

"Thanks, Talmadge," Jimmy said. "I gotta go. Blackie's getting ahead of me."

There was silence in the living room. Elizabeth Anne began to giggle. "Chiggers," she gasped. "Chiggers!"

Granny chuckled. "Well, maybe that'll account for his unusual movements. Maybe."

Jimmy's voice cut into their laughter. "Blackie! Blackie! Wait up!"

Hiram hastily turned the volume down. "I can see this is going to be a long day," he said. "Pull up a chair."

They settled down with drinks and cookies. Elizabeth Anne had been given the job of writing down Jimmy's remarks. Trying to keep a straight face, she wrote in the first ones.

"Are you sure she has to write down everything?" Granny asked.

"Sometimes mysteries are solved by one overlooked clue," Hiram replied. "Sometimes it is something that has been overlooked for years. In this case, for a great many years."

He and Paul spread out a map on the coffee table. Paul's job was to track Blackie's movements by marking the places on the map. He made the beginning mark at the beach path. He thought about where Talmadge's plot was. He made a careful mark. Then he connected the two dots.

Jimmy's comments into the bug dwindled as he began to have fun. Still, his chatter to Blackie kept them informed about what was going on. The two investigated a crab and then let it go. They checked out the tide pools left by the receding water. Then they climbed out on the rocks down by the restaurant. The room was suddenly filled with the angry squawks of pelicans.

Granny sat bolt upright. "He's playing on those rocks again! One slip and he'll fall!"

Elizabeth Anne and Paul looked at each other, wide-eyed. Jimmy had been warned not to play on the breakwater. But Blackie was chasing pelicans and Jimmy was chasing Blackie. He had forgotten all about rules.

"He forgot, Granny," Elizabeth Anne said. "He wouldn't disobey."

"He won't forget for long," Granny said.

She marched to the phone and dialed the restaurant's number. The children could hear part of a conversation with Charley, the manager. A few minutes later, a big voice boomed into the receiver.

"Hey! Hey, Jimmy! Your Granny said to get off those rocks!"

"Yes, sir," came the startled reply.

A few minutes later, Jimmy's whisper was back. "Sorry, Granny. I forgot."

"Well, you'd better not forget again, young man," Granny answered. Then she realized that

Jimmy couldn't hear her. She threw up her hands. "I'm going to get some mending," she said. "This thing is driving me out of my mind."

The next hour or so was filled with Jimmy's play. Elizabeth Anne and Paul got bored, but Granny and Hiram listened. "I'd forgotten what it was like to be a boy," Hiram said. "Jimmy is bringing back good memories."

"I know," Granny said. "I've been that length of sand almost every day for fifty years. And for the last thirty, I haven't seen half of what Jimmy has seen today."

"He does wake you up," Hiram agreed.

"Hey, here's a big shell," Jimmy said loudly. There was silence for a few minutes. Then a roar of booming static burst into the room. They all jumped. A moment later it stopped, and Jimmy's voice came back. "Did you hear the ocean?"

Granny rubbed her ears. "I think we just listened to the inside of a conch shell. And Jimmy's heartbeat."

"Where is he now?" Paul asked.

"Let's see. He passed the restaurant. He must be near the amusement park now," Hiram answered.

Paul made another mark on the map. "Blackie's heading in a straight line right down the beach," he said. "Other than the climb on the rocks, Jimmy isn't making any side trips. This is going to wash out."

"Maybe," Hiram said. "You didn't expect it to work right away, did you?"

Paul frowned. "Well, yes. I did."

"Relax." Hiram sounded confident. "Something may happen yet."

"I wish it would hurry up," Elizabeth Anne said. She stretched her legs. "Jimmy is having all the fun. Hey, why can't we go with him tomorrow?"

"When only Jimmy's with him, Blackie does more wandering," Hiram explained patiently. "He knows Jimmy will follow."

Paul was grinning. "So the dog isn't with Jimmy. Jimmy is with the dog. I thought there must be a reason that Blackie likes Jimmy best."

The receiver boomed again, but this time it wasn't Jimmy's voice.

"Hey, kid!"

Everyone in the room swung around to look at the receiver.

"You stay away from Blackie," Jimmy's voice said.

"Aw, come on, kid," the other voice said. It had a strange, coaxing tone.

"Is that the man who took Blackie?" Paul asked.

"Sounds like him," Granny said. "I'm calling the police."

"Keep listening, kids," Hiram said. "I'm going down there."

"Wait for me," Granny called. She finished speaking and put the phone down. "I'm going too!"

Chapter Ten
The Chase

Still on the beach, Jimmy forgot all about the bug in his pocket. He began to back away from the man. Jake had called him "Bill."

"Get away," he said again.

When Bill grabbed for Blackie, the dog turned and ran into the crowded amusement park. Jimmy was right behind him. Blackie whipped in and out without bumping anyone. Jimmy was not quite as good. In his effort to keep Blackie in sight, he stumbled against a large man. Popcorn showered around them.

"Hey, kid," the man shouted. "Watch out, will'ya?"

Jimmy yelled back over his shoulder, "Sorry!"

He didn't stop. Blackie was too far ahead. Jimmy was just in time to see a black tail disappearing under the counter of a Ring-toss booth. Jimmy scrambled under the counter.

"Get out of here," the attendant snapped. "Crazy kids!"

He grabbed a broom and started thrashing at Blackie. "Git, dog!"

Blackie panicked. He tried to go over the back. One leap landed him in the "duck pond." He slipped in the water. The ducks went down, one by one. Then one last leap took him under the canvas curtain at the back. He was out and gone.

Jimmy rolled back under the counter and headed around the booth. He looked frantically about. Blackie was nowhere to be seen. Then he saw the wet tracks. They led straight down the boardwalk. Jimmy groaned. The tracks were right where Bill could see them, too.

Jimmy looked back quickly. The stringy-haired man was still shoving his way through the crowd. Jimmy turned and ran.

Jimmy caught up with Blackie. There was nowhere to hide, and the wet tracks had left a clear trail. Jimmy dragged the protesting Blackie along by the collar. Without a leash, he found it hard going. Then Blackie tried to go one way around a baby stroller and Jimmy tried to go the other. The baby screamed and the mother frowned.

Jimmy had to let go. Then there was nothing he could do but chase Blackie again. Blackie skidded to a stop beside the Ferris wheel. It had stopped to let passengers out. Blackie wagged his tail.

"Hi, Black," the operator said. "How're you doing, boy?"

"Can we go up?" Jimmy asked eagerly.

"Black too?" The man's eyebrows raised.

"I'll pay for him," Jimmy said. "Just take us up."

The operator shrugged. "Okay, but you hang on to him!"

Jimmy dug in his pocket. He pulled out a wad of string, a dinosaur eraser, a piece of crayon, and some pebbles. The operator was getting impatient.

"Hey, kid," he said.

"I've got it!" Jimmy dug in the other pocket. He pulled out a rumpled dollar and handed it to the man. "Keep the change," he said.

"Thanks," the man replied. "Up you go!"

Jimmy took one last glance backward. Bill was only twenty steps away. Jimmy darted into the seat, pulling Blackie with him. The bar slammed down. The seat swung up. Jimmy stared down into Bill's dark, angry eyes.

Bill pulled out some change and shoved it at the operator. He stepped into his seat. Quickly Jimmy pushed Blackie over the edge of theirs. Then he jumped after him lightly, landing on his feet.

The operator of the Ferris wheel gave him a surprised look. He glanced from Jimmy to Bill. Then he winked. With his usual "Up you go!" he started the motor. This time he didn't stop for another passenger. The stringy-haired man went up and up to the very top. Then the operator stopped the wheel.

Bill turned to look at the seat where he expected to see Jimmy and Blackie. Jimmy heard his outraged yell clearly. So did the operator.

"Better get going, kid," he said.

Jimmy grabbed Blackie. "Thanks," he said.

"Sure. You need me to call the cops?" the operator asked.

Jimmy shook his head. "Just leave him up there a while if you can."

"This machine has a few kinks in it," the operator said. "Hangs up like this every once in a while."

Jimmy laughed. He and Blackie headed down the boardwalk. "Thanks again," he called back.

Then all his attention was on Blackie. The dog was moving eagerly through the crowd again. It was almost as if he were going a regular route.

"Hey, Blackie," Jimmy said. He remembered what Hiram had said about the amusement park. "Do you come this way all the time?"

Blackie wagged his tail. He stopped at an ice-cream booth. The attendant spoke to him. Then she saw Jimmy.

"I never saw you with Black before," she said. "He's usually a loner."

"I'm staying for the summer," Jimmy said. "Does he come this way all the time?"

" 'Most every day," the lady replied. "Likes my ice cream."

"Ice cream? Blackie?"

"Sure," said the lady. She dropped a scoop on a paper plate and put it down for Blackie. He slurped it up greedily. "Want one?" she asked Jimmy with a smile.

"How much?" he asked. He didn't have much money left after paying for the Ferris wheel. Thinking of the money made him look back. The man was still stuck at the top.

"It's on the house," replied the lady. She chuckled. "Any friend of Blackie's is a friend of mine."

"Thanks," Jimmy said. He accepted a strawberry cone. He licked it and watched the Ferris wheel while he waited for Blackie to finish.

When the dog was ready to move on, the lady was busy with other customers. She waved as they left.

Blackie went around the other booths and headed down the beach. The amusement park was planning to expand in this direction. Construction work had already begun under the pines. Blackie led Jimmy past the bulldozers and cranes. They scrambled down and then up the sides of a drainage ditch.

Jimmy looked behind them. No one was following. He breathed a sigh of relief. "Guess we lost him, Blackie," he said. Suddenly he remembered the bug. He turned his head and spoke loudly toward his pocket. "We lost him."

When Blackie stopped to dig, Jimmy sat down to rest. The sea breeze whispered in the pine needles. Overhead, squirrels ran back and forth, chattering at Blackie. Blackie barked and gave chase. Jimmy sat still and watched. The black dog flashed in and out of sunlight and shadow, chasing the squirrels. They raced across the limbs above him. Blackie ran until he was tired. Then he trotted back to Jimmy and sat down to rest.

"So this is how you stay in shape," Jimmy said. He nodded in approval. "Good exercise."

Blackie tried to lick Jimmy. Jimmy dodged. "Whoa," he said. "I'm hot enough."

Blackie got up and trotted to the edge of another ditch. He looked back at Jimmy and whined. Then he disappeared over the edge. Jimmy followed.

At the bottom, Blackie was digging in the sand. Jimmy scrambled down. "What'cha got, Blackie?"

Blackie whined and looked up. Then he made a quick, stiff-legged jump. He nudged something with his nose. A loud chattering from above made him back off. A squirrel darted down the tree. He stopped on a rotted piece of wood and faced Blackie.

Jimmy grinned. Whatever Blackie had, the squirrel wanted. Both made several darts forward and then back. Finally the squirrel made a quick leap forward and retreated with what looked like a nut in its mouth.

Blackie gave chase, barking furiously. Jimmy blinked. The nut had looked awfully big. He glanced overhead. There were no trees with nuts on them. A sudden suspicion sent Jimmy tumbling down to the bit of wood. That nut had been the size of Blackie's clay ball!

Chapter Eleven
Pegleg's Treasure

Jimmy knelt beside the broken pieces of wood. Whatever they had been part of, it had rotted away. Jimmy dug in the sand beside the pieces. His fingers touched something solid. He pulled it up. It was an old iron hinge.

Excitement swept through Jimmy. "This is it!" he yelled. "Blackie! This is it!"

Hurriedly, he dug some more. Sand scattered under his probing fingers. He dug up an iron clasp and another hinge before his fingers closed on something round. Jimmy pulled it up and shook off the sand. It was another clay ball.

Before Jimmy could open it, a dark shadow fell across the sand. Jimmy looked up. The stringy-haired man stood at the edge of the ditch. His eyes glittered.

"So you found it."

The words were quiet, but they sent a chill down Jimmy's spine. He looked around for Blackie. Slowly he began to back away from the remains of Pegleg's chest.

"How did you find me?" he asked.

Bill grinned unpleasantly. "There's a great view from the top of a Ferris wheel," he answered. "But I don't need you anymore. Just move away from the treasure."

Jimmy backed up to the other edge of the ditch. The man scrambled down. He fell to his knees and dug frantically in the sand. He was so intent on digging that he didn't hear the sirens. Jimmy backed farther away. When he reached the edge of the trees, he saw people running. They were running toward him.

He stood still and waited, clutching the ball behind him. He heard Bill give a wild cry of

disappointment. "There's nothing here!" he said. "Nothing at all!"

The policemen reached the ditch, guns drawn. Jimmy stared across at them, wide-eyed. Granny and Hiram caught up with the policemen and ran across the ditch to Jimmy. The other men and women from the amusement park stopped and stared at the man in the ditch. Someone said "treasure," and excitement crackled in the air.

Granny held Jimmy close. They watched as the people surged past the line of policemen and began to dig in the sandy ditch. One policeman led Bill away. The others watched the diggers, shaking their heads.

"So that's it, Jimmy," Hiram said. "Nothing left at all."

Slowly Jimmy held out his hand. "There was one."

Granny took it gingerly. "We'll check it later. We'd better get home now, son."

Blackie came scampering back. His tongue was hanging out and his eyes were sparkling. He jumped up on Jimmy.

"Huh," Jimmy said. He hugged the dog. "Just where were you when I needed you?"

They made their way across the ditch and through the trees. Before Jimmy reached the boardwalk, he looked back at the trees. The squirrels ran back and forth in the trees, scolding the diggers below them. Jimmy grinned. "Take good care of Pegleg's treasure," he whispered.

Paul and Elizabeth Anne were waiting on the porch. They ran to meet the small group that straggled up the path.

"Jimmy, are you all right?" Elizabeth Anne hovered over him.

He waved her away and scrubbed the cheek she had kissed. "Don't smother me! Sure, I'm okay!"

Paul grinned. Elizabeth Anne did tend to mother a person. He walked along by Jimmy. "So you found it," he said. "There really was a Pegleg."

"Reckon so," Jimmy said. He had developed a swagger. "Me and Hiram knew it all along."

Hiram grinned. He straightened his old slouch hat and strutted beside Jimmy. "You bet," he said.

Even Jimmy laughed. They went back into the house in a good mood. They gathered around the kitchen table. Granny took out the clay ball. She used a kitchen mallet to crack it gently. The clay crumbled away, and a ruby gleamed on the polished tabletop.

Hiram held it up to the light. "A pigeon ruby."

"A what?" Jimmy said.

"A pigeon ruby," Hiram repeated. "A big ruby. It's worth a lot of money."

"We'll take it down to the museum tomorrow," Granny said. "I'm just glad it's over. Those diggers and their holes will be gone forever."

"When do we get the money?" Elizabeth Anne asked. "I want to go shopping."

"You don't," Granny said, smiling. "You children are minors. The money goes to your parents."

The children looked at her, dismayed.

"Don't worry," Granny said hastily. "I'm sure it will go into your college fund."

"But where did the rest of the treasure go?" Elizabeth Anne asked at last. "What could have happened to it?"

"Yeah," Paul said. "It had to go somewhere."

Jimmy didn't say anything. He fidgeted.

"Maybe people picked them up over the years and never said anything," Hiram guessed. "Or maybe old Pegleg took it back. Maybe the two stones got overlooked."

Jimmy opened his mouth. Then he shut it again.

"Or maybe they got scattered and buried when the ditch was dug," Granny suggested. "If so, we'll know soon. That crew of people were really digging by the time we left."

"The squirrels have it," Jimmy said in a small voice.

"I know," Elizabeth Anne said. "A hurricane washed them away. Maybe they *are* lying out there on the beach, just scattered by the water."

"The squirrels have it," Jimmy said, more loudly.

There was silence at the table. All eyes turned to Jimmy. "What?" Hiram said.

"I said the squirrels have the clay balls," Jimmy said. "They look like nuts, y'know."

Hiram's eyes went round. "You mean it?"

He began to laugh. Elizabeth Anne giggled. Granny sputtered, and then she too began to laugh.

Paul just kept on staring. "You mean—in all those trees—there are hoards of rubies—"

"And diamonds," Elizabeth Anne gasped.

"And emeralds," Granny said, wiping her eyes.

"Well, that's a squirrelly idea, if I ever heard one," Paul said indignantly. He frowned when everyone burst into laughter again.

"Listen, everybody! That means there's still a fortune out there. All we have to do is go get it," he pleaded.

"I don't want to."

Jimmy's blunt statement brought silence back to the table. He looked at the others sadly. "I wasn't going to tell you at all. I don't want

Pegleg's treasure any more. I want our beach back."

"I agree with Jimmy. The holes can be filled," Granny said. "But if the search goes on, the trees will be chopped down in order to find the jewels."

"You mean if we tell about the squirrels," Elizabeth Anne said, "people will do the same to the trees that they did to our beach? And besides, what would happen to the squirrels?"

"People act funny when they are hunting treasure," Jimmy said, shivering. "They'd probably shoot them. And somebody might take Blackie again. Blackie's more important than any pirate's treasure."

Granny and Hiram smiled at each other. Hiram coughed. "Well," he said, "I've had my fill of treasure hunters. A body can't even go shelling without a gaggle of gold hunters breathing down his neck. What about you, Paul?"

Paul looked from one to another. His eyes stopped on the ruby. "I think the fun was in the chase," he said slowly. "The hunt. Now we know where the treasure is, I'd just as soon leave it there."

Granny's smile grew. "Am I to understand that you don't want to collect the jewels?"

The other four looked at each other. Solemnly, each one held out his hand. They did a four-hand shake. They spoke at the same time.

"Let the squirrels have it!"

And that's just what they did.